THE ARABIAN NIGHTS
CHILDREN'S COLLECTION

Dados Internacionais de Catalogação na Publicação (CIP) de acordo com ISBD

J76s   Jones, Kellie
        Sinbad the sailor / adaptado por Kellie Jones. – Jandira : W. Books, 2025.
        168 p. ; 12,8cm x 19,8cm. – (The Arabian nights)

        ISBN: 978-65-5294-172-5

        1. Literatura infantojuvenil. 2. Contos. 3. Contos de Fadas. 4. Literatura Infantil.
        5. Clássicos. 6. Mágica. 7. Histórias. I. Título. II. Série.

2025-605   CDD 028.5
                                                                                           CDU 82-93

Elaborado por Vagner Rodolfo da Silva - CRB-8/9410
Índice para catálogo sistemático:
1. Literatura infantojuvenil 028.5
2. Literatura infantojuvenil 82-93

The Arabian Nights 10 Book Collection
Text © Sweet Cherry Publishing Limited, 2023
Inside illustrations © Sweet Cherry Publishing Limited, 2023
Cover illustrations © Sweet Cherry Publishing Limited, 2023

Text based on translations of the original folk tale,
adapted by Kellie Jones
Illustrations by Grace Westwood

© 2025 edition:
Ciranda Cultural Editora e Distribuidora Ltda.

1st edition in 2025
www.cirandacultural.com.br
No part of this publication may be reproduced, stored in a retrieval
system, or transmitted in any form or by any means, electronic,
mechanical, photocopying, recording, or otherwise, without written
permission of the publisher.
This book is a work of fiction. Names, characters, places, and incidents
are either the product of the author's imagination or are used fictitiously,
and any resemblance to actual persons, living or dead, business
establishments, events, or locales is entirely coincidental.

Sinbad the Sailor

W. Books

Long ago, in the ancient lands of Arabia, there lived a brave woman called Scheherazade. When the country's sultan went mad, Scheherazade used her cleverness and creativity to save many lives – including her own. She did this over a thousand and one nights, by telling the sultan stories of adventure, danger and enchantment.

These are just some of them ...

Sinbad
A rich and famous sailor from Basra

The Porter
A porter in Baghdad

The King of Cassel
The king of an island in the first voyage

The Jewel Merchant
A clever trader in the second voyage

Captain Pavan
The captain in the third voyage

King Usman
The king of an island in the fourth voyage

The Old Man from the Sea
A strange man in the fifth voyage

The King of Sri Lanka
The king of an island in the sixth voyage

Caliph Harun al-Rashid
The ruler of Baghdad

The Ivory Merchant
A trader in the seventh voyage

Chapter 1

The Story of the Porter and the Sailor

Once, in the great city of Baghdad, there lived a lowly porter. The hottest day in summer found him sweating under a heavy load, which he was carrying from one end of the city to another. He was tired, hungry and thirsty.

Finding himself in a quiet street where the pavement was sprinkled

porter
A person whose job is to transport goods from one place to another.

with rose water, the porter stopped and put down his burden. Feeling a cool breeze blowing against him, he chose to sit awhile.

The breeze carried scents from a huge house nearby, exotic woods and incense mixing with the rose already perfuming the air. Then came the scents of food and the sounds of feasting. From an open window he could hear music and voices and fun and laughter and – was that a nightingale?

While the porter tried to identify what kind of bird was singing so

incense
A substance that makes a nice smell when burnt.

prettily, a servant came out of the house.

'Who lives here?' the porter asked him.

The servant, who was dressed more magnificently than any servant the porter had ever seen, laughed.

'Who lives here? *Who lives here?* How can anyone in Baghdad not know about Sinbad the Sailor?'

'Oh,' said the porter. Because of course he knew about Sinbad the Sailor, the famous voyager who had sailed around the world. He had just never seen his house before. Now he looked at it again and could not help feeling jealous. Sinbad was rumoured to be the second richest man in Baghdad, while the porter often thought of himself as the poorest.

When the servant had gone, the porter looked to the heavens and sighed loudly. 'Almighty Creator, how different are the fortunes of Sinbad and I! He lives his life in pleasure; I live my life in hard work. He dines on the best food every day; I have barely enough barley bread to last the week. Why give him so much and me so little? What have I done wrong?'

While the porter was thus complaining, the well-dressed servant reappeared.

'My master wishes to speak to you,' he said, and motioned the porter to follow him inside the house.

Inside the porter saw what he had

only smelt and heard outside. There was a table covered in all manner of dishes, from savoury to sweet, and surrounded by all manner of guests, from all over the world. Sat by an open window was a handsome older man. He had white teeth set within a wide smile, and a white beard neatly trimmed around a weathered brown face.

It was Sinbad the Sailor.

The porter, who had been shaking with nerves, was suddenly frozen with fear. What should he do? He did not belong here, in this place, with these people. He was just a porter!

Or did the sailor perhaps want him to deliver something?

Sinbad spoke to the person nearest to him, and that person immediately stood up. Sinbad waved at the chair and the porter realised that he was telling him to sit in it.

'Um …' the porter began.

But then the servant was pushing him forward and round and down – and then, suddenly, the porter was sitting next to the second richest man in Baghdad.

'Um …'

The servant brought him coffee in the tiniest cup with the tiniest spoon, and the porter drank just to avoid saying "Um" again.

'Welcome to my home,' said Sinbad. 'Please help yourself to some food – I promise you will find it better than barley bread.'

The porter almost spat out his coffee. The sailor must have heard

his complaint through the window!

'I beg your pardon,' he said, 'I have no excuse for my words except my tiredness.'

'Calm yourself,' said Sinbad. 'I am not angry. But tired or not, I believe you meant what you said. And I want you to know that what pleasure I take from life now is because I worked hard for it in the past. Do not think that I am simply lucky. Luck has had little to do with it.'

The sailor raised his voice so that the other people in the room could hear it.

'In fact,' he said, 'now seems like a good time to tell the story of how I came by my riches. Would you all like to hear it?'

There was a chorus of yeses – and one 'Um'.

'Very well,' said Sinbad. 'Prepare yourselves for an adventure ...'

Chapter 2
The Story of the First Voyage

I am from Basra in Iraq, and in my home my father was a well-known merchant. He spent his life earning a great sum of money, which I spent within a year of his death. Afterwards I fell upon hard times and decided to earn my fortune as my father had earnt his. I joined a merchant ship when I was sixteen

---
merchant
Someone who buys and sells goods.
---

and set sail towards India and the scattered islands of the ocean.

I was so seasick in those early days that I can barely remember them. I went from swaggering on land to barely being able to stand up on the ship. I think the other merchants enjoyed seeing my confidence brought down a peg or two!

We stopped at several islands where we sold or exchanged our goods. For me those goods were Persian rugs, which I knew a lot about from my father. Other merchants dealt in silks, spices, oil,

Persian rugs
Valuable, handwoven rugs traditionally made in ancient Persia, now called Iran. Still popular today.

tea, medicine, precious stones, exotic woods – you name it.

One day the wind left our sails, and we were forced to make an unplanned stop at an unknown island that was barely above water. We left the ship and made our way to the shore in rowing boats. As we approached, the island looked so flat that it was almost like the water gave way to a meadow of grey-green seagrass.

On this island the other men rested, but I could not. Usually I used our time on land to eat and drink as much as I could to replace what I lost at sea due to seasickness. On this island, however, my sickness continued. Since I could not rest, I walked. It was only a small island, longer than it was wide. To distract myself, I counted my paces from end to end: '... one hundred and sixty, one hundred and sixty-one, one hundred and sixty-*two*.'

I noticed that the edges of the island were wet despite the fact that there were no waves.

Then I counted my paces from side to side: '... one hundred and eighteen, one hundred and nineteen, one hundred and—'

Suddenly I stumbled and lost count. It was almost as if the island had moved, but I told myself that I was simply weak from seasickness.

I re-counted: '… ninety-four, ninety-five, ninety-*six*.'

I had reached the opposite side again and somehow the island had gotten smaller. It was not just seasickness knotting my belly, it was worry. Something was not right.

'Let us go back to the ship,' I said when I returned to my shipmates.

'First we need to collect drinking water,' they said lazily.

'There is nothing here,' I told them.

'Coconuts, then.'

'There is nothing here!'

At my shout, the island really did move. All of us stumbled, even the most experienced sailors with sea legs that could keep them steady during storms. I stumbled into a hole that swallowed my whole foot.

'Back to the ship!' the other men yelled.

As I tried to free my foot, they raced back to the rowing boats.

'Come on, come on, come on!' I hissed, and tugged furiously at my ankle.

Suddenly it was free and I was

flying backwards. A jet of warm water shot out from where my foot had been. The men were in the boats now, rowing furiously back to the ship.

'Wait for me!' I yelled, beginning to pound after them. But the island moved again. I was running, then paddling, then swimming.

This was no island! It was a whale. And it was *diving*.

As the whale disappeared from under me, I clung onto a barrel that we had brought on land to fill with water. I do not think I would have been strong enough to stay afloat without it. The other men had made it back to the boat and the wind had returned with them. I did not know if they had failed to realise that I was gone or if they simply did not care. Either way, they set sail without me.

With the wind came the waves. I was at their mercy for the rest of

mercy
To be in a situation where something or someone has complete power over you.

that day and the following night.
When I was ready to let go of the
barrel and die, a wave threw me onto
a new island. This one stood much
higher than the last. I had to use the
roots of trees to climb up the bank
and out of the water.

All I wanted to do was sleep, but
I was dangerously thirsty. Luckily
I did not have far to go to find a
delicious water spring that I believe
saved my life.

I went deeper into the island and
found a plain of grass where a horse
was grazing. I will admit, I do not
know what I wanted more in that

moment: to ride the animal to safety or to eat it. Drifting in the sea for so long had cured me of my sickness. For the first time in weeks, the thought of meat – any meat – did not make me want to empty my stomach.

As I came closer, I saw that the horse was a magnificent animal, worth a small fortune. I had wasted enough money in my life to know this.

I was running my hand over the animal's back when a knife pressed into my own.

'What do you want with the king's horse?'

The voice from behind me was gruff and old. I tried to relax despite the knife.

'May I turn around?' I asked.

'Slowly.'

I turned to find a man even older than he sounded.

'I meant no harm,' I said. 'I have been drifting at sea for days and washed up on your island only hours ago.'

'It is not *my* island,' said the man. 'It is called Cassel, and it belongs to the king. I am one of his grooms, out exercising his horse.'

groom
Someone who looks after horses as a job.

I eyed the knife still in his hand. 'Are you sure you are not one of his soldiers?'

The man chuckled but did not lower his knife.

'I am unarmed.' I held my arms out at my sides, although my ragged clothes could not have hidden a needle, let alone a sword.

Satisfied, the man put away his knife. He listened as I told him what had happened to me. In fact, he enjoyed the tale so much that he agreed to take me back with him to the palace.

---

unarmed
To be without a weapon.

'You must tell the king your story!' he said.

The island was small and so was the palace, but the king's heart was big. He was so shocked by my misfortune that he let me live with him in comfort. But I had learnt my lesson well: I did not want to waste time like I had once wasted money. I wanted to be a merchant like my father, but my goods were on the ship that had left me. I would have to start building my business again.

Cassel was a good place to do that.

Many people came and went there on ships from all over the world. They traded, or collected supplies, and I collected knowledge. I dined with the king and his guests every night, and I was always asked to tell the story of the disappearing island, even though everyone knew it by now. In return, I heard stories from foreign courts and distant lands. I learnt about the history, politics and laws of places I had never heard of.

I visited the port every day hoping to hear news from Basra, or to find an opportunity to return there, but

port
A town or city with direct access to water, where ships can load and unload passengers and goods.

I was not unhappy. I grew into a man, tall and strong and bearded. Then one day I went to the port and saw a familiar ship. It was the one that had left me to die in the sea. On the wall alongside it I saw a familiar bundle too.

'I can offer you a good price,' a voice said. It was none other than the captain of the ship. 'Would you like to take a closer look?'

He does not recognise me, I thought.

I nodded in answer and he rolled out the Persian rugs I had collected on our former travels together. I was surprised that he still had them.

'Are they yours?' I asked, hoping that my voice had changed as much as the rest of me.

'No,' he admitted. 'They belonged to a boy named Sinbad who was lost at sea.'

'Lost?' I said. 'Or abandoned?'

The captain frowned. 'What do you mean?'

'*I* am Sinbad. As you can see, I am not lost, and I will not pay for goods that already belong to me.'

I could see the captain thinking back to the Sinbad he had known, from cocky boy to sickly merchant.

Neither image seemed to fit the man before him.

'I do not believe you,' he said finally.

I grabbed a passing fisherman I knew and asked him, 'What is my name?'

'Sinbad?' Surprise turned his answer into a question.

'How did I get here?' I asked next.

The fisherman smiled more confidently. 'You mistook a whale for

an island until it swam away. The sea carried you here.'

'Thank you.'

I let the fisherman go and turned back to the captain. He was wide-eyed with astonishment.

'It really is you!' he said. 'Sinbad!'

Hearing my name, the rest of the sailors and merchants from the ship came over. They had to cover my beard with their hands to recognise me.

'We thought you were dead!' they all said, until I had to believe that it was true. They had not abandoned me. They simply had not seen me clinging to the barrel. And they had felt so bad about my fate that they had not been willing to sell my rugs until now.

'Here,' said the captain. 'Take them back and come with us. We are sailing home.'

Persian rugs were much rarer on Cassel than where I am from. I was able to sell them for a very high price, but I gifted the best to the king for being so kind to me.

He then gifted me with nutmeg, cloves, sandalwood, pepper and ginger. They were goods that were local to the island and not worth very much there. But back home they were rare enough to make me a rich man.

And they did.

In the huge house in Baghdad, on the street sprinkled with rose water, Sinbad fell silent.

After a moment, the porter said, 'Um …'

Sinbad nodded for him to ask his question.

'So is that how you made your fortune? From sandalwood, cloves and ginger?'

'Oh no,' the sailor smiled. 'That was only the beginning ...'

Chapter 3

The Story of the Second Voyage

I did not stay in Basra long before I became restless. I decided to move to Baghdad, but even in this great city I found myself longing for something more. Whereas once the tilting decks of a ship had felt wrong to me, now the steadiness of land did. I wanted to go to sea again.

My second voyage started in a similar way to the first, minus the

seasickness, plus extra money.
We traded from island to island,
and I was the most successful of our
crew. But the more the customers
liked me, the less my fellow
merchants did.

One day we landed on a large
island with all kinds of fruit trees,
but not a single person or animal.
We walked in the meadows, and
along the streams that watered
them. Some of us picked the flowers
and plucked the fruits. I myself sat
down near a stream between two
high trees that provided thick shade
from the sun. I ate and afterwards

fell sleep. I cannot tell how long I slept for, but when I awoke the ship was gone. And this time there was no question that I had been abandoned by my jealous crew.

Alone on that island, I bitterly regretted setting sail again. Why had I not been happy with the riches from my first voyage? Why did I always want to do and be and see and have *more*?

'Because you are greedy,' I said, answering my own question. 'Now your greed has made enemies of your friends.'

When I was done blaming myself,

I blamed the others: 'How could they just leave me? I cannot help it if people would rather do business with me than with them.'

Then I reminded myself not to waste time on regret *or* anger, because time, after all, is more precious than anything.

I used my next minutes to climb the tallest tree on the island and see if there was anything that would give me hope of escape or rescue. When I looked towards the sea, I saw nothing but sky and water, but looking over the land, I saw a white shape in the distance. A building, perhaps?

I set out briskly towards it after stuffing my bag with fruit from the trees. As I drew nearer, the white shape became bigger and bigger. Eventually I saw that it was a large dome on top of a hill. When I climbed the hill and touched the dome, I found that it was smooth and warm.

I counted fifty paces around it and could find no opening like a door. When I rapped my knuckles against it, nothing happened – there was no answer, at least from inside the dome. Suddenly, the sky went black. At first I thought that it was a cloud, but instead of passing above me, it descended towards me.

'Craaaaaw!' it shrieked.

That was when I knew that it was not a cloud. It was a *roc*: a bird so huge it could carry off an elephant as easily as a worm. I had heard sailors speak of them and never believed until that moment that they were real. Now I would have my own story to tell – if I survived. Because the creature was still descending. Any moment it would be upon me.

I dove behind the dome and hid. The world got darker and darker – and then a warm, feathery softness covered me.

'Craw,' said the roc. And then it was silent.

Enough time passed that it was safe to say the bird was not hunting me after all. It was not hunting anything. It was nesting.

The white dome was an egg.

Slowly, my panic faded, and I

started thinking. As the roc shifted to a more comfortable position on its egg, a leg thicker than the tree trunk I had climbed earlier appeared from the feathers.

If I tie myself to its leg, I thought, *wherever it goes, it will take me with it.*

My sash was too short, so I took the turban off my head and unrolled it to its full length. While the roc dozed, I bound us together good and tight around my middle.

I spent an uncomfortable night like that, but in the morning I got to fly, so it was worth it. To see the world from above like a bird is something

I will never forget. Far, far below me the egg become a dot and the land become a blur. When I could see it clearly again it was because we were diving so close to a mountain range that I thought we would crash into it. Jagged spikes threatened to spear me before the roc stopped suddenly and perched on a ledge. Despite the danger, I took the chance to untie us. I had unwrapped half my turban when the roc flew off again, and I had to clasp my arms around its leg to keep from falling. The bird arrowed towards the ground with its legs – and me – outstretched. Talons the length of my forearms shot out.

The biggest, longest snake I had ever seen came into view. The roc snatched at it and missed. The snake reared up. The roc wheeled round. They faced off again, one above, one below, and me between. I was close enough to hear the snake hiss and see the venom dripping from its fangs. Close enough to jump to the ground – which I did.

I landed hard on the ground and rolled away, pulling the turban fabric with me. The roc sank its talons into the snake and the snake wrapped its jaws around the roc's leg where I had just been. I watched them fight from a distance, sometimes dodging the tail end of the snake's long body. When it stopped thrashing, I knew that the roc had won. It began ripping into the snake with its beak and eating it. It was a gruesome sight, so I quickly slunk away, retying my turban as I went.

I was in a valley between mountains so high and steep that I could not climb out. All I could do was walk and hope that the valley would open out eventually. As I kept my eyes on the distance, however, all I continued to see was an endless channel littered with stones.

Should I go back to the roc? I wondered. *Try to tie myself to its leg again and go somewhere else?* As if in answer, a shadow swam over me. I looked up to find the roc already flying away. In an instant it was so far off that it looked like a regular-sized bird on the horizon. I kicked a stone in frustration as I realised I was stuck there.

I should have stayed by the fruit trees, or even the roc's nest, I thought. *Better yet, I should have stayed in Baghdad!*

I lifted my foot to kick another stone and froze. With a gasp, I picked the stone up and turned it over. The edges were veined with black, but the heart flashed green in the sunlight. I had never traded in them, but I knew an emerald when I saw one – even rough and raw like this one was.

I cast about looking for more emeralds, but the next coloured stone I found was red (a ruby). Then blue (a sapphire). Then a yellowish-gold I did not know the name for. My hands and then my arms filled with a whole rainbow of stones, and I kept finding more. I had only one small

leather bag to put them in and that still held fruit from the island, so it was soon full. When I could not squeeze the rest under the sash around my waist, I tucked them under my turban.

I went on to find diamonds as clear as spring water, and a gold nugget so large I needed both hands to lift it. I was deciding how to carry it when I realised that no amount of gold or jewels would mean anything if I died in that valley. My waterskin was almost empty and I was no closer to finding an exit.

waterskin
A container for holding water that is usually made of sheep or goat skin.

I forced myself to put the gold down and walk faster. I did not stop no matter what other treasures I saw. And as night fell and darkness crept into the valley, I stopped being able to see anything.

For a while I walked blindly, waiting for the moon to take over from the sun. I could hear strange noises around me – a sort of dry, dragging sound. My feet caught against something solid, but not as solid as rock. The moon finally shone down – and illuminated a nest of snakes.

Many of the snakes were the same

size or bigger than the one the roc had eaten – meaning they were more than big enough to swallow me whole. Only these snakes, it seemed, were smart enough to hide from the roc during the daytime. Now that it was night, they were coming out.

They seemed almost as surprised to see me as I was to see them. Their tongues flickered towards me curiously at first, and then again with a hiss. The moment they reared their heads, I ran, even though there was nowhere to go. From behind me came a soft, slithering sort of thunder as the snakes followed.

The valley shook and stones trickled down the mountainsides. I dodged left and leapt right to avoid them. Up ahead I saw a large boulder begin to fall and half hoped that I would be there in time for it to crush me. I did not know how to make myself stop running, but I knew that I could not escape. I was going to die one way or another – and the boulder seemed like the better way.

But the boulder never landed. I watched it catch on a ledge similar to the one the roc had perched on, but lower down. Was it low enough for me to reach?

Either it was or fear gave me wings. As I reached the bottom of the ledge, I jumped so high it felt a little like I was flying again. I seized one handhold and then another, and finally pulled myself onto the ledge. There I prepared for a second uncomfortable night.

Once again, I could not sleep. The ledge was so low that I feared the largest snakes would reach it. They certainly tried. All night I fended them off as they stretched and lunged towards me. I threw rocks that had collected on the ledge. Many hours later, I had developed perfect aim, but I was down to my last stone. With it I shot a final snake out of the air as it uncoiled like a spring. I thought about throwing the jewels I still carried but they were smaller, and I was tired. It was time to accept my fate. I closed my eyes and waited for the snakes to reach me.

I heard them writhing below the ledge. I imagined the mass of their bodies spilling over it towards me. And then I felt the warmth of the sun against my face. It was morning! Light crowded the shadows from the valley, and I looked down to see only the ground and its covering of jewels. The snakes had fled back to their dens to wait until nightfall again. But I would not wait with them.

I climbed down from the ledge and continued walking along the valley. I was so tired that I barely saw the jewels that covered the ground. I simply dragged my feet through them and kept moving.

At noon I let myself stop and rest. I was sitting with my back against the mountainside, eating the last of the fruit from my bag, when I heard a loud *splat*.

Raw meat the size of a dead sheep rolled across the ground in front of me and settled. *How strange,* I thought.

Splat.

Another landed over to my right.

Splat. Splat. Splat.

Now raw meat was landing *everywhere*, but never the same place twice. I looked up and thought I saw a person on top of the mountains. But then I saw something else.

'Craaaaaw!'

It was another roc. Or the same one. And I had the same idea: *If I tie myself to its leg,* I thought, *wherever it goes, it will take me with it.*

First it would have to land, but that was easy. It was already circling the meat. As another piece fell, the roc dived and caught the piece in its beak. Then it landed on the valley floor to seize not one, not two, but *three* more pieces in each foot.

There was no chance to tie myself to its leg. There was no chance to even take off my turban! The roc raised its wings to fly off and I ran towards it, throwing myself at its leg. Just like that, I left the valley.

I did not know for sure whether this roc was the same one as before until it took me to a different nest at the top of a mountain. This nest had two eggs. The roc laid down the pieces of meat, opened its beak and was just about to eat when a dozen men appeared. They ran towards us shouting and waving their arms. The roc was so startled that it flew off without the meat.

'What are you doing here?' one of

the men demanded when he saw me. 'This is *my* nest so those are *my* jewels.'

I realised then that the meat was studded with jewels after landing on the valley floor.

'What do you mean this is your nest?'

'I mean that each merchant has his own and this one is mine. And so are any jewels the roc brings back to it.'

'Are you saying,' I asked, 'that because you cannot go into the valley and get the jewels yourself, you and other merchants are using meat as bait so the rocs bring them to you?'

'Why do you care?'

'Because you have saved my life with your cleverness!'

The jewel merchant's rudeness vanished. 'You mean you are not here to steal my jewels?'

bait
Something, usually food, that is used to attract animals or fish so that they can be caught.

'I have jewels of my own! I have been to the valley myself.'

'Impossible. There is no way in or out.'

'Except by roc,' I said. When he still looked doubtful, I pulled out the biggest diamond I had found in the valley and gave it to him. 'This is for saving my life,' I added.

Seeing that I had indeed been into the valley and must have a story to tell, the merchants invited me to stay with them at their camp. But first I helped them to pluck all the jewels that had stuck to the meat. We left the meat behind for the roc.

At the merchants' camp I told my story and they told theirs. I learnt that they came to that island every year during the roc's nesting season to get the jewels they needed to trade.

'But I am a merchant, too,' I said. 'Why have I never heard of this practice?'

'Would you have believed it?'

'No,' I agreed. And perhaps my listeners will not either.

I stayed with the jewel merchants until the roc eggs hatched and the parents could no longer be frightened from their nests. Then I set sail with them for the Isle of Roha. There

I exchanged some of my jewels for goods to trade, including camphor from the camphor trees that grow there.

After stopping at many other places, I returned to Baghdad a richer man than ever, even after giving much money to the poor. With no need to go on any more voyages, I decided to live my life comfortably and peacefully.

camphor
A white solid with a cooling smell that comes from camphor trees. It can be used on skin as medicine to help treat pain or itching.

In the huge house in Baghdad, on the street sprinkled with rose water, Sinbad fell silent.

After a moment, the porter asked, 'And did you?'

'Did I what?'

'Live your life comfortably and peacefully?'

'Indeed, I did,' Sinbad said. 'For a while …'

Chapter 4

The Story of the Third Voyage

I soon grew bored of living a comfortable, peaceful life and set sail on another voyage.

After stopping at several ports, our ship was caught in a terrible storm. It lasted for days. By the end of it, our captain, whose name Pavan meant 'wind', told us we had been blown far off our course.

We reached an island where men

crowded the shore. There must have been a hundred of them and only twenty of us. They wore ragged clothes and were of many different ages from many different countries. Something in the hungry way they watched us made me afraid.

'Must we stop here?' I asked.

'It is either that or we sink here like the others,' Captain Pavan replied.

'What others?'

He pointed at the skeleton of a ship in shallower water. My eyes found more wrecks nearby.

The captain was frowning. 'Shipwrecks must happen here often. I do not want to stay any more than you do, but the ship is damaged from the storm. We will fix it and be on our way.'

That was the plan, and we were so focussed on our task that we did not notice when the figures vanished from the shore. When I looked again, I saw a hundred heads in the water, swimming swiftly towards us.

'Ambush!' I shouted, but it was too late. The ragged men, who were shipwrecked sailors, climbed the hull and crowded the deck. They soon overpowered our crew. Afterwards they seemed to discuss what to do with us. I say 'seemed to' because they spoke a language that was made out of many languages. I recognised some words, but not others.

It did not matter. I knew that the ship was overcrowded so I was not surprised when they threw us overboard. I was just grateful that they did not kill us first.

We swam to the island they had just fled and watched them sail away in our ship. I had been stranded twice by now and had found a way to escape each time. I believed I would find a way again. Plus this island was covered with fruit and coconut trees, and there was drinking water everywhere. We would not die of thirst or hunger.

On the very edges of the island, we found huts and caves and treehouses where the shipwrecked sailors must have lived. Further into the island, we found a huge building. I do not mean that it was like a palace, because the rooms in a palace are smaller than these were. I am saying that each room was the size of a house. And if that was not worrying enough, we found a huge pile of bones in one of them, beside a huge firepit for roasting large animals on.

'We should leave,' I said, already backing up the way we had come.

'Look!' said one of the other merchants.

The open door behind us was now blocked by a giant. He was as tall as a palm tree with ears the size of the largest fronds. He had only one eye in the middle of his forehead, but it was the size of a well and twice as deep. It glowed red. His nails reminded me of the roc's talons, and his equally long front teeth stuck out

---

frond
The wide, spreading leaf of a palm, fern or similar plant.

strangely from his mouth. Now
I saw why the shipwrecked sailors
had wanted to escape so badly!

The giant saw us and lifted me in
one hand. He studied and squeezed
me until I thought my eyes would pop
out of my head. Frowning he put me
back down and seized Captain Pavan.
While I was tall and lean, the captain
was short and fat. The
giant licked his lips
and looked pleased.
I realised that the
roasting pit was not
for cooking large animals on. It was
for cooking humans!

Luckily, we did not see him roast or eat the captain. The giant locked us in a cage outside his house. Each mealtime he would look through the bars with his glowing eye, then reach in with his big hand and take another one of us out. Soon there were only seven of us left, including all the thinnest merchants whom the giant tried to fatten with meat from the island. We were too afraid to eat any of it, of course. He brought the food to us on the same rod of metal he planned to cook us on! Usually, he would pluck the meat off with his giant fingers and drop it through the bars. But one day he simply threaded the whole rod through the bars and left it there.

The rod was long and sharp for skewering meat. It gave me an idea.

The next time the giant came to look through the bars for his next meal, I drove the rod into his eye.

The giant, who had been carrying a wooden bowl and spoon, jumped back, screaming. In his pain, he threw the bowl and spoon, which hit the side of our cage and broke it. The prisoners raced out and fled back towards the shore. Only I stood still.

'Wait!' I called after them. 'We should bring the bowl with us!'

'Why?' they shouted back.

'What else are we going to sail in?'

We did not know how long the giant would be blinded for so we had to hurry. Together we lifted the bowl – which I feared would not be big enough for all seven of us – and carried it towards the water. At the last minute, I added the spoon.

Behind us the giant continued screaming, and then the earth started shaking. We soon discovered that there were other giants on the island, who were now running to help the first.

We made it to the water, waded in with our 'boat', but then the giants arrived and started throwing boulders at us. Two more of the men were killed. Finally, when the water was deep enough, the remaining five of us climbed in. We paddled with our hands and the spoon. Eventually we passed out of the giants' long reach.

But sailing a bowl is a difficult thing, and the waters in those parts were often stormy. We soon found ourselves at the foot of huge waves. A strong wind made the bowl spin round and round dizzyingly. As night fell, we tried to cling on, but by morning I was the only one left, and the spoon had snapped in half.

As I continued to paddle with one of the pieces, I became aware of a dark shape swimming in the water below me. I was not worried at first – this was the sea, after all.

But then whatever it was snatched the broken wood from my grasp. It disappeared under the water, then bobbed up again some distance away. I grabbed the other half of the spoon and tried to paddle with that. Once again it was seized, only this time I did not let go. I managed to raise the creature's head out of the water and saw that it was a giant sea serpent.

Angrily the serpent wrapped its body around the bowl, turning it over and throwing me out. It wrapped around me next and pulled me down, squeezing and squeezing until all the air had left my lungs.

Then I remembered the broken end of the spoon still in my hands. I drove the splintered end into the serpent, stabbing it the same way I had stabbed the giant. The serpent let go. Just as my lungs felt like they would burst, I reached the surface and could breathe again.

I tried to pull myself onto the capsized bowl but the bottom of it

capsized
When a boat has turned upside down.

was too slippery to grasp. I did not know if the sea serpent was dead or still circling, but I knew that death was near either way.

'Hello?' I heard a voice call. Then I heard the same word said in several other familiar languages. I looked up to see the shipwrecked sailors calling to me from the ship they had stolen. They had seen the battle with the sea serpent, but when they hauled me aboard and heard (and translated) the battle with the giant, they were even more amazed.

A man who was also from Basra said that I could travel with them and keep the goods I still had on the ship. Most of the sailors left at the first port and the ship became less crowded. I stayed on, visiting several islands with them. One of these islands was Salabat, where sandalwood is grown and made into medicine. From there we went to another island where I also stocked up on cloves, cinnamon and other spices.

At last, after another long voyage, I returned to Baghdad with more wealth than I could count. I gave a great deal of it to the poor again and used some to buy this very house we are in now.

It has been my favourite place to live ever since.

In the huge house in Baghdad, on the street sprinkled with rose water, Sinbad fell silent.

After a moment, the porter asked, 'So you stayed here after that?'

'Do you mean in this house or in Baghdad?'

'Both,' said the Porter

'Neither,' said Sinbad. 'I soon went on a fourth voyage …'

Chapter 5

The Story of the Fourth Voyage

After I had rested from the dangers of my third voyage, I travelled overland to Persia, visiting many new places. Eventually I set sail from a port in the Persian Gulf.

There was such a strong wind at our backs that the captain sent his men to take in the sails before they could be shredded. But the men were blown from the rigging and many others off the decks. The sails did not tear, but a great cracking sound told us that the whole mast was breaking off. After that we were side-on to the waves and another cracking sound told us that the hull was breaking up too.

As the ship sank, many of the merchants and sailors were drowned and all of the goods we carried were lost. I and five others drifted on a raft of wooden planks to an island.

rigging
The ropes, cables and chains on a boat or ship that control the sails.

mast
The long, upright pole on a boat or ship that supports the sail and rigging.

This island was not deserted
like the one on my second voyage
had been. Nor was it inhabited
by giants like the one on my third
voyage. The people who lived there
were men and women like you and
I. But I soon discovered that this
did not make them any less likely
to eat us than the giants had been.

Forgive me, I am jumping ahead
in the story ...

To begin with, our hosts were
very welcoming. *Too* welcoming.
We spoke different languages,
but we understood each other
by making signs with our hands.

When our hosts held their hands to their lips, I understood that they were inviting us to eat. The six of us did not need to be asked twice. We followed the locals back to their village and my companions began eating a wide range of foods, including rice prepared with coconut oil so that it was extra fatty. But no meat or fish.

I nibbled at the rice, sensing that something was not right. Why were our hosts not eating too? All they did was watch as my companions greedily devoured the rice and everything else. Then my companions began to act strangely, almost as if they were sleepy, and yet not too sleepy to eat. Realising that the food must contain something that made them sleepy, I began to eat even less of it so that I could keep my senses.

This went on for days. While my companions got fatter, I got leaner. Then they began disappearing as the locals took them away one by one. Again, I never saw them being eaten. But the absence of any meat at the table made me wonder if the island had no more animals left to hunt or fish to catch.

Perhaps that was what had made our hosts into cannibals.

When my companions were all gone, the cannibals had no interest in me. I had grown too thin and sickly to eat so I was left to wander the village freely. I pretended to be sleepy from the food they still gave me, but all the while I looked for a way to escape without being noticed. When I wandered close to the village edge one day, an old man made a noise and waved his hand to call me back. The younger men and women were away somewhere, and

---

cannibal
Any animal, including humans, that eats its own kind.

I knew that I might not get a better chance than this. So I ran away.

With no way to escape the island, I tried to stay hidden. Over the next few days, I ate properly, restoring my strength with coconuts, plants that were safe to eat and wild green vegetables. Pepper grew all over the island – something I had traded in before and was very valuable in certain places. With riches like that, I was not surprised when a merchant ship stopped near the island and a few men with axes and swords rowed ashore.

I guessed from the weapons that they already knew about the cannibals.

'Oh yes,' the leader confirmed, speaking Arabic. 'We know about them. I am amazed you are still alive!'

'So am I,' I replied.

'Well, as soon as we have gathered enough peppercorns, you must come home with us. I am sure our king would love to hear about your adventure.'

Their king was King Usman. When I met him soon after, he reminded me of the King of Cassel from my first voyage.

The island King Usman ruled over was a wonderful place, and I was welcomed by everyone – especially the king. It made me feel very guilty because as wonderful as the island was, I longed to return to Baghdad, and I would need his permission to do so.

To ease my guilt and prepare my request, I thought about what I could give King Usman as a gift. The island had plenty of everything, from food to people, but it only had two horses. Both belonged to the king, who rode them bareback.

'Why do you not use a saddle?'
I asked King Usman one day.

'What is a saddle?' he answered, so that is what I decided to give him.

I went to a workman with a design for him to make the shape of the saddle, which I covered with velvet and leather. Afterwards I went to a blacksmith and had him make my design for a bridle and some stirrups. When I presented all three to the king, he was delighted. Then I showed

him how to use them and he was even more pleased.

'Let us go for a ride together,' he said. I agreed thinking that it would be a good opportunity to ask about leaving.

I had never ridden without a saddle before but I refused to let the king lend me the one I had made specially for him. We rode on in a comfortable silence while I worked up the courage to speak.

'You know, Sinbad,' he said suddenly. 'I always regretted not having any children. But I have come to look upon you the same way I believe a father must look upon a son.'

I almost fell off my horse. 'Y-you flatter me, Your Majesty,' I stuttered.

'Since you came,' the king continued, 'I have been a happier man. I hope that you will stay forever.'

'Well, actually, Your Majesty—'

'I know that you do not have any family in Baghdad, so I wish for you to take a wife from among my people. I know just the woman. She has been in love with you since you arrived!'

How could I refuse such a request, after such a compliment? The answer is I could not. I was married soon after to a rich noblewoman.

On the very day of my wedding, the

wife of the man who found me on the island of cannibals suddenly fell sick and died. His name was Emir and we had become good friends. I went to comfort him.

'May your wife rest in peace and may God grant you a long life,' I said.

Emir shook his head sadly. 'My life will not be much longer than my wife's was. It is the custom here for husbands to be buried with their wives and wives buried with their husbands when they die.'

custom
A way of doing something that is generally accepted for a certain group, setting or time period.

'You mean buried *alive*?' I gasped. Emir nodded.

And that was exactly what happened. The dead woman was dressed in her richest clothes and jewellery for the funeral, and then lowered into a pit on a wooden platform. After her, poor Emir followed with a waterskin and a loaf of bread on a platform of his own. Finally, the pit was covered over with a large stone. I was horrified! Especially when, only days later, my own wife sickened and died of the same illness.

King Usman loved me and I was

not from the island, so I told myself that he would not make me follow the same custom and be buried alive. But I was wrong. With tears in his eyes, he watched with the other islanders as I was lowered after my wife into a second pit. Then a stone sealed me inside.

With the little light that crept in around the edges of the stone, I was able to see that the pit opened out into a large cavern at the bottom. I could also see the waterskin and the loaf of bread beside me on the platform. As first I was determined to ignore them and let myself die sooner. But when I was hungry enough and thirsty enough, I could not stop myself eating and drinking.

I noticed that the corner of my bread was missing, as if someone or something had already eaten it. With nothing else to do, I placed the last piece of bread on the ground and watched until a rat appeared to eat it. Then, finding that the bread was now small enough to carry, the rat ran away with it. I followed, curiously, into the darkness. I already knew that there were parts of the cavern that were like passageways leading to nowhere. At one such dead end, the rat disappeared. How could I see that in the dark, you ask? Because daylight was leaking through the bottom of the wall, between the gaps in a pile of stones where the rat had gone. I moved the stones to reveal a small hole and, behind it, *sand.* I could even hear the sea!

Using my hands, I made the hole deeper by digging down into the soft ground. I could not make it any wider because the wall around it was solid rock. It was not wide enough for my shoulders to fit through widthways, but if I could turn sideways, I thought I might just be able to get my head and chest through.

Do you see this scar on my forehead? And this one on my chest? *That* is how close I came to not making it. I lost more skin than I care to remember squeezing through that hole. But on the other side was daylight and freedom. I found myself on a beach, and I think I swallowed half of it in kisses as I rolled across the sand in relief.

Soon after I saw a merchant ship that must have just left the port on the other side of the island. I used the bright red fabric of my turban to alert the crew that I needed help. They in turn sent a small rowing boat to pick me up and were happy to take me with them once they heard my story.

I joined them on their journey to the Isle of Bells, which is about ten days' sail from Sri Lanka with a regular wind, and six days from the Isle of Kela, where we also landed. We traded for lead, sugar and camphor. I say 'we' but you may wonder what I had to trade by that time, having lost all my goods in the storm that sank my ship.

Well, I am ashamed to admit that before I left the burial cavern, I removed my wife's jewellery from her body – and she was a rich woman. There was a lot of it. This earring is all that remains of a pearl necklace she wore at our wedding. I did not love her, but I remember her in my own way.

Eventually of course, I returned to Baghdad, where I decided never to set sail again.

In the huge house in Baghdad, on the street sprinkled with rose water, Sinbad fell silent.

After a moment the porter asked, 'And did you?'

'Did I what?'

'Ever set sail again?'

'Oh,' said Sinbad. 'Well, of course I did …'

Chapter 6

The Story of the Fifth Voyage

I began to reason with myself that although my other voyages had taken terrible turns, that did not mean another one would. In fact, surely there could be no more strange adventures to have after I had already had so many.

With this logic, I decided to set sail a fifth time. But first, I would buy my own ship. That way, I would not be left behind by accident or on purpose, and I would not stop anywhere I did not want to. Storms were not something I could control, but I would always keep an eye on wind and sail.

The ship was built and I loaded it with goods to trade. I agreed to take several other merchants and their goods too. Then I hired a captain.

The first island we stopped at held a familiar sight: it was another roc egg. Only this one was beginning to hatch, and a giant baby beak was already breaking through the smooth white dome. Before I could stop them, the merchants who sailed with me had cracked the egg the rest of the way and killed the bird inside it.

'This will be enough to feed all of us!' they said.

'I wish you had not done that,' I said, watching the sky nervously.

The captain agreed with me. 'Since you *have* done it,' he added, 'we should go back to the ship quickly.'

But the merchants were already building a fire to cook with. They refused to leave until after they had eaten, and by then I could see another familiar sight: it was the roc parents returning. They approached with a terrifying 'CRAAAAAW!' that grew even louder when they saw the empty egg and dead baby bird. It was enough to make the merchants finally start running back to the ship.

I was surprised when, instead

of coming after us, the roc parents disappeared. But by the time we had returned to my ship, they were back. In their talons they carried boulders. They started dropping them over us as we set sail. Our captain managed to dodge the first, but the second hit us directly, tunnelling straight through the deck and out of the hull at the bottom. Then we were sinking. But the boulders kept falling, crushing everyone on deck, almost crushing me. When they had no more boulders left, the rocs flew away.

Once again, I was alone and adrift

at sea. Only this time I washed ashore within hours and not days. What can I say about the new island that I have not said about previous ones? It was like a giant garden. There was grass, where I rested, fruit, which I ate, and water that I drank. Oh – and there was a half-naked man sitting on the bank of the stream.

At first I thought that he must have been shipwrecked too, and I wondered how long he had been on this island – because he was very, *very* old. When I spoke to him, he did not answer. Instead, he pointed at my back, and I understood that he wanted me to carry him. I wondered if perhaps his legs did not work, but then he jumped onto my back before I had even agreed. His legs certainly *did* work! They wrapped around my waist so strongly that they threatened to break by ribs. Meanwhile the grip his arms had around my neck threatened to choke me. From there he pointed across the stream.

'Do you want me to carry you to the opposite bank?' I gasped out. He dropped his hand, which I took for a yes, then he brought it back to my neck.

I carried him across the stream and immediately fainted on the other side from a lack of air. When I came around, the old man was still sitting on top of me. He yanked at the end of my turban as if he was steering a horse, forcing me to stand up. Then he pointed towards some ripe fruit trees and dug his heels in my belly to drive me forward. Using my turban again, he made me stop.

He rode me from tree to tree and ate as much as he wanted. He did not get off my back all day, and when I lay down to rest at night, he held onto my neck and lay down beside me. In the morning he pinched me awake and made me carry him again. It was awful!

After a few days of this, the old man steered me to a tree that was heavy with dates. That fruit grows near the top of the tree so he had to climb onto my shoulders to reach it. He plucked several dates, stretching up until he wobbled, and threw them down to me. One by one I caught them. Then he began to throw so many that my hands were quickly full. I had no choice but to juggle them. I threw them high, tossed them round, and the old man stopped fruit picking to watch. Round and round, round and round, they went, until I could feel the old man swaying on my shoulders.

Is he getting dizzy? I thought. I carried on juggling in case I was right.

Round and round, round and round–

Thud.

The old man fell off my shoulders and struggled to stand up again.
I did not wait for his world to stop spinning. I ran for the beach, and there I met the crew of a ship collecting water.

'That was the old man of the sea!' they said when they had heard my story. 'No one has ever escaped that man's clutches. Not unless they died first.'

Their captain was also impressed with my story. He let me sail with them to the harbour of a great city, where the houses hung out over the sea. One of the ship's merchants who had befriended me invited me to go ashore with him.

'But I have nothing to trade,' I said. 'All my goods were on my ship.'

'Take this,' he replied, giving me a large sack. 'And go and fetch some pebbles from the beach.'

'I cannot trade *pebbles*!' I said.

'Trust me,' he replied.

So I went and gathered some pebbles. Afterwards my friend

introduced me to a group of people carrying similar sacks and told me to go with them.

'They will show you what to do,' he called after me. 'Just make sure you stay with them.'

The group led me into a thick forest where coconut trees grew. They were the tallest coconut trees I had ever seen, and their trunks were so smooth that they could not be climbed. And you would not want to climb them, either, because a great many monkeys lived in them.

As the humans gathered at the bottom of the trees, so the monkeys gathered at the top. When there were almost as many monkeys up there as coconuts, one of the merchants threw a pebble at them. The monkeys, in turn, threw coconuts back in revenge. And so it continued until the ground was covered in coconuts and the monkeys were furious.

Was tricking monkeys into giving me coconuts to sell my favourite way to earn money? Far from it. But one sack of coconuts became two and two became four, and I was soon able to start trading again.

From there we sailed to the Isle of Comari, where the best woods used for perfume, incense and small carvings grow. I exchanged my coconuts for these woods and for pepper. Afterwards I hired divers to go diving and bring me up me some pearls that were large and pure. In this way, I recovered the fortune I set out with and then some, I returned home to Baghdad and a well-earnt rest!

In the huge house in Baghdad, on the street sprinkled with rose water, Sinbad fell silent.

After a moment the porter said, 'So, in the end, even after buying your own ship, the voyage still went wrong?'

'Terribly wrong,' Sinbad agreed, plucking a date from his table.

'The life of a sailor is dangerous indeed!'

'Incredibly dangerous.' Sinbad threw the date into the air and caught it in his mouth.

'But I do not think you were finished with that life yet, were you?'

Sinbad chewed … and smiled …

Chapter 7

The Story of the Sixth Voyage

It is true – by now the urge to set sail was so deep in my blood that even five shipwrecks could not flush it out. But for my sixth voyage, I decided to avoid the Arabian Sea where so much unluckiness had occurred. I travelled overland once more, through Persia and on to India, then set sail from a new port.

The ship I chose was bound for

a long voyage, but after a time our captain became lost. This only became worrying when we saw him leave the ship's wheel, throw off his turban, pull at his beard and begin beating his head like a madman.

'What is the matter?' I asked him. 'The weather is fair, the wind is good, the ship is fast and the men are happy. We are lost, yes, but we will find our way – I always have in the past.'

The captain, who knew my history, said, 'I understand what you are saying, Sinbad, but understand *me*: these are the most dangerous waters in any ocean. Here the current is so strong that no ship can escape its pull. They are carried somewhere that no ship has ever returned from. In fifteen minutes, we will all be dead!'

The captain ordered the sails to be lowered, but he was right: it was not the wind moving us forward now, it was the current. The ship was carried to the foot of a cliff, where she struck and smashed to pieces. Surprisingly, however, no one died, and we were able to save most of our food and goods. Other shipwrecks

current
The direction and flow of water.

had not been so lucky. At the foot of the cliff there were the splintered remains of many other ships and countless skeletons. And with them lay an incredible amount of goods and riches of all kinds.

Walking over the wreckage of wood and bone, we made our way around

the foot of the cliff to a long beach backed by mountains. The sea there was also littered with shipwrecks and glittered with gold and jewels. But the land was full of riches too. The wood that grew there was just as good as the wood that grew on the Isle of Comari, where I visited on my fifth voyage. There was even a freshwater stream that flowed into a cavern made entirely from diamond. On top of that, there was a sort of spring that came from a volcano underwater, spitting bitumen in a steady black stream into the sea. In return the sea

bitumen
A natural, sticky black liquid or semi-solid, now used to make road surfaces.

sent back lumps of ambergris.

In short, there was enough on that island and in its waters to make every man there rich forever, but absolutely no way to leave with any of it. We were trapped. Those who tried to swim away were washed back, often injured, sometimes dead. The men who did not die then died later. We each had equal shares of food from our boat, and they did not last long. One by one, men died, until I was the only one left.

ambergris
A grey stone made in the bellies of whales. It is used in making perfumes due to its sweet smell.

I moved to live close to the river, away from the many graves of my shipmates that now covered the beach. While I still had enough energy, I dug my own grave on the bank of the river. Afterwards I intended to lie down and die in it, but the sight and sound of the river flowing alongside me gave me an idea.

I said to myself, 'This river, which runs in a cavern underground, must lead somewhere. If I make a raft and float down it, I will leave this place the same way the river does. Either it will take me somewhere safer or

I will still die. Either way, I will not lose anything by trying.'

Using planks of wood from the shipwrecks, I made myself a good, strong raft. Then I collected as much treasure as it could carry. There were diamonds, emeralds and exotic woods, but I took mostly ambergris because it is so light that it would not weigh down the raft.

I paddled down the river with two oars until I was too tired. Then the current carried me into the cavern. The ceiling was so low that I had to lie down on the raft like I had planned to in my grave. For a while it felt like I really had died, because it was too dark to see anything and I was too weak from hunger to move at all. I do not know how long I slept or where I travelled. The next thing I knew, the sky was above me again andmy raft was tied up somewhere I had never been. I was surrounded by men talking loudly in a language I did not know, and there were so many of them that I was afraid.

'Stay back,' I said.

My voice was as weak as my body, but the men had no wish to hurt me. One who spoke Arabic reassured me, 'We are men of Sri Lanka. This river comes from the neighbouring mountain to water our fields and crops. It has never before brought a man with it. Will you tell us how you came to be here?'

'Please ...' I croaked. 'Food ...'

I was quickly fed and soon recovered enough to tell my story. After he had translated it for his friends, the man who spoke Arabic said, 'If we had not plucked you from the river ourselves, we could not believe such an incredible story. You must tell it to our king yourself, else he will not believe it either.'

They immediately sent for a horse and helped me to mount it. Walking ahead with my belongings, a few of them led me to the capital of Sri Lanka, which is an island I mentioned on my fourth voyage but did not visit. I was presented to the king who invited me to sit near him and tell my story again. Afterwards the men who had brought me showed the king my belongings. The king's eyes widened at the sight of the diamonds and emeralds.

'I have no choice but to believe your story,' he admitted. 'Those stones are some of the most beautiful I have ever seen.'

'Then they are yours, Your Majesty. Please take them with my blessing for your kindness.'

The king shook his head. 'Here in Sri Lanka, you do not have to buy our kindness, Sinbad; it is freely given. I will not take your wealth. Let me instead try to add to it before you leave us.'

The king ordered one of his officers to look after me during my stay. He saw to it that I was sheltered and fed. My goods were taken to my room, and every day I visited the king for an hour. He wanted to know about where I was from and who ruled it. The rest of my time was spent exploring the capital of Sri Lanka.

The city stood in the middle of the island, at the end of a valley, surrounded by mountains so high they can be seen from three days away at sea. All kinds of rare plants and trees grew there, especially cedar and coconut. There was also a pearl fishery in the mouth of its main river, and rubies and sapphires in its valleys.

When I was strong enough and had satisfied my curiosity about the place, I asked the king if I could go home. Alongside his permission, he gave me some of the pearls and sapphires his country is most famous for. All the king wanted in return was for me to deliver a letter once I returned to Baghdad. The letter was written on a rare animal skin and read:

> To Caliph Harun al-Rashid, from one who commands a hundred elephants and whose palace overflows with a hundred thousand rubies. I send you a small gift as a token of my friendship.

The 'small gift' was a cup carved out of a single ruby, that was thirty centimetres high, two and a half

---

caliph
A spiritual or religious leader in Islamic countries.

centimetres thick and filled with pearls. There was also the skin of a snake with scales like pure gold, which the king explained, 'If a person lies on this, they will be protected from sickness.' Lastly, there were thirty grains of camphor as big as pistachio nuts.

As promised, I took this gift home to Baghdad and immediately presented it to Caliph Harun al-Rashid. When he had read the King of Sri Lanka's letter, he asked me, 'Is this king truly as rich as he says?'

I bowed to the floor a second time, rose and replied, 'Commander of the Faithful, I believe he is. I did not see inside his treasury, but his lands are rich indeed. When he leaves his palace – which is as magnificent as he says, he sits in a throne on top of an elephant. Before him rides an officer carrying a golden lance. Behind him rides another officer carrying a golden rod. On the top of the rod is an emerald fifteen centimetres long and over a centimetre thick. In public he is always surrounded by a guard of a hundred men, all richly dressed and–'

treasury
A place where money and other valuable things are kept.

But here the caliph held up a hand. I bowed a third time and stopped talking.

'That is enough,' he said, 'I am very pleased to be in contact with the king of such a country. Is your name Sinbad?' I confirmed that it was. 'I believe I have heard of you.

Indeed there is a rumour that you are almost as rich as I am.'

I began to assure him that this could not be the case, but he held up his hand again and I stopped. 'I do not believe this was your first voyage, was it, Sinbad?'

'No, Sire.'

'And have you encountered other rulers on your other travels?'

'Yes, Sire.'

'Tell me about them …'

That is how I came to the personal attention of the Commander of the Faithful. And by then, yes, people had begun to say that I was almost as rich as he was. Though I cannot say if they were right. I only knew that I had more than enough.

In the huge house in Baghdad, on the street sprinkled with rose water,

Sinbad fell silent.

After a moment the porter said, 'Enough? So you were ready to stop sailing for good?'

'I was.' Sinbad nodded

'And trading? What about your work as a merchant?'

'I did not need to work. I was already nearly as rich as our great caliph. Plus I was much older than I had been when I began my first voyage. My beard was grey, my body was tired. These stories have taken hours to tell but they took years to live.'

The porter finally realised how long he had been there.

'My parcel!' he cried, jumping up from his chair. 'I was meant to deliver it hours ago!'

'One of my servants delivered it for you,' Sinbad reassured him. 'Sit back down.'

'But ...' the Porter sat slowly. Now that the spell of Sinbad's words had been broken, he was back to feeling like he did not belong there. 'But ... the story is over,' he pointed out. 'I should leave.'

'Not yet,' Sinbad said. 'The story is not over yet. There was still one more voyage to be had ...'

Chapter 8

The Story of the Seventh Voyage

As I have said, I was tired. And I was finally ready to be bored and lazy. It was not long, however, until Caliph Harun al-Rashid summoned me to the palace.

'I wish for you to take my reply to the King of Sri Lanka,' he told me.

My shoulders sank and I dared to say, 'Commander of the Faithful, I beg you, please choose another man to deliver your message. I have decided never to go to sea again.'

'You are the one who introduced him to me,' the caliph said; 'therefore you are the one who must introduce me to him.'

I had no choice but to obey, and I left the palace with all the gold I would need to pay for the journey. As soon as the caliph's letter and present were delivered to me, I departed. And I am happy to say that I arrived in Sri Lanka without any misadventures.

The king was delighted to see me. 'Sinbad!' he said. 'Welcome back.

I have often thought of you since you left.'

I thanked him for his kindness and delivered the gift from Baghdad. The caliph's letter said:

> To the King of Sri Lanka, from the Commander of the Faithful and the servant of God. I received your letter with joy and send you this in return. I hope that you will look upon it as my warm acceptance of your offer of friendship.

The caliph's present included clothing made from the finest materials, such as cloth from Egypt and even real gold. There was a large bowl carved from colourful agate stone, the bottom of which showed the image of a man with a bow and arrow aimed at a lion. Lastly, he had sent a rare tablet carved with words said to have come from King Solomon, the wisest man who ever lived.

The King of Sri Lanka was very pleased and kept me on the island for longer than I wanted. When I managed to leave at last, unfortunately my return journey was not as easy as the outward one had been. Within four days, the ship was attacked by pirates. Any merchants and sailors who fought back were killed. I did not fight back, so I lived.

The pirates took us to an island where they sold us as slaves. I was bought by a rich merchant who dressed and treated me well. We did not speak the same language,

but one day he brought me a bow and arrow, and I understood that he was asking if I knew how to use them. I showed him that I did by shooting the fruit from a tree. He looked pleased.

Afterwards he signalled that I should sit behind him on his elephant, which we rode into the jungle. When we were far from town, where the trees were thickest, he signalled that I should climb one of them. This was easy, for there was already a ladder attached to the tallest tree, and a platform at the top to sit on.

Again, the merchant looked pleased.

When I tried to climb down, however, the merchant handed me the bow and arrow and some food, then quickly removed the ladder. I understood that I was to stay up the tree. The merchant pointed between the bow and his elephant, and then he rode away, leaving me behind.

Although I did not know the reason for it yet, I did not mind the time alone. It gave me time to think. As day turned to night, I thought about Baghdad, and how, after seven eventful voyages, there was nowhere in the world I wanted to be more than my own home. I had been a free man my whole life, but only now that I was a slave did I understand the true value of that freedom. I had always thought that time was the most valuable thing. But now I saw that freedom was even more valuable than time. For I would rather live one day as a free man than a whole year as a slave.

These thoughts were interrupted when the trees around me began to shake as if a strong wind blew through them. But the air was still. A tremble passed from the ground all the way up to the top of my tree. A loud, trumpeting sound announced the arrival of a herd of wild elephants who came to graze below me.

The oldest and largest of them was almost as tall as my perch, with thick white tusks the size of my legs.

The moonlight shone on them, and on the arrows that lay at my feet. And I understood what I had been left there to do.

I had not asked the merchant what goods he traded in, and he would not have understood me if I had. The answer, I knew now, was ivory.

Ivory, which is the tusks of elephants and other animals, used to make ornaments, dagger handles and other things far less beautiful than the animals themselves.

My 'master' wanted me to kill these animals, so that he could cut off their tusks and trade their ivory.

I felt sick at the thought, but ivory was not new to me. Somehow seeing those elephants, witnessing their wildness, envying their freedom, made killing them for their tusks unthinkable. I suppose it is similar to eating meat and finally sparing a thought for the animals it comes from. Right then, I was looking the animal in the face, and I was suddenly reminded of the time I had thrown stones at monkeys for coconuts during my fifth voyage. I should have chosen differently then. I *would* choose differently now.

It was the only freedom I had.
I kicked the bow and arrow from
my perch. As it fell to the ground,
the largest elephant
noticed me, trumpeted
a warning and the
herd moved away.

In the morning, the merchant returned and saw that I had not killed any elephants. He was not pleased. He gave me the bow and arrow back, this time with no food. I understood that I would have to kill an elephant or starve. So I kicked the bow and arrow away again and chose to starve.

Each night the elephants visited my tree and left unharmed. Each morning the merchant returned and left displeased. If I was lucky it rained in the meantime and I could drink the rainwater.

The largest elephant began to

watch me as I watched her. Her eyes were clever but kind. One night I pulled down the untouched branches that were out of even her long reach. She tugged the leaves free greedily with her trunk and fed them into her mouth. The next night she brought me a mango as if to say thank you. The night after that she brought bananas. The merchant could not understand how I was still alive.

Finally, the elephant let me touch her. Her skin was warm and rough, her trunk gentle as it touched me in return, tugging at my clothes. She seemed to want to move me, but she could not quite wrap her trunk around my middle. She stood underneath my platform instead, her hairy grey back a short drop away, and waited until I had climbed on. At her trumpet, the herd left my tree and took me with them.

They carried me even deeper into the jungle, so deep that we neared the opposite side of the island. They stopped at an elephant graveyard that would have made the ivory merchant richer than he could ever dream. I climbed down onto a mound of elephant bones, teeth and tusks. I did not know what to do until my elephant friend passed me one of the tusks. It felt heavy and wrong in my hands. I did not want it, but I needed it to buy my freedom. And somehow the elephant knew. With one last trumpet, she and the other elephants left. I never saw them again. Nor did I ever forget.

I used the tusk to buy passage on a ship.

'This is too much!' the captain said.

'Too much and not enough,' I replied. 'Take me home safely, and we will be even.'

So he did. I returned to Baghdad and paid my respects to the caliph. When he heard of my final adventure, he heaped even more riches upon me, but I had stopped caring about such things.

From then on, I cared only about friends and family. I traded in kindness not coin. And I was richer than I had ever been.

In the huge house in Baghdad, on the street sprinkled with rose water, Sinbad fell silent for the final time.

After a moment the porter said, 'You were right. Luck has had little to do with your life. You have worked hard for what you have. You deserve to enjoy it, and may you live a long and healthy life to do so.'

'Thank you,' said Sinbad. 'You are always welcome to enjoy it with me, and to sit at my table. I rarely leave home these days.'

'But do you not miss it?' the porter asked him. 'Your old life, I mean? It was dangerous, yes, but also exciting. I know this city like the back of my hand, but the rest of the world is a mystery to me.'

'Really?' Sinbad said. 'Then have you ever thought of becoming a sailor?'

'No,' the porter admitted.

'Perhaps you should. I own several ships you could sail on.'

'But where would I go?' the porter wondered.

Sinbad smiled. 'I recommend everywhere …'